I0746445

Frank Mercer

In

THE
MERCER
FILES

The Girl in the Crimson Coat

Phillip Deam

The Girl in the Crimson Coat
Introduction:

They say every city's got a heartbeat; this one bleeds instead.

Some cases change you. Some dames ruin you. She walked into my life in heels and red velvet, looking for a missing girl.
But the deeper I dug, the more I realized.
It wasn't about what was missing.
It was about what she already took.

This is the story of the girl in the crimson coat.
And the moment I stopped being a man looking for justice.
And became one running from it.

Chapter 1:
The Knock and the Photograph

Every city's got a pulse, this one just forgot it was supposed to beat

Frank Mercer

The sound of rain tapping against the office window hit harder than the pounding in my skull. Last night's bourbon was doing its best impression of a marching band.

Some cases you chase. Others land in your lap like they were dropped from heaven, still smoldering from the fall. And this one? This one came wrapped in red silk and smoke—long before I knew her name.

Rita cracked the door open to say something, but she didn't get the chance.

The woman walked in as though the room had been waiting for her.

Heels like gunshots on hardwood, sharp, certain, unapologetic.

She didn't pause.

She didn't ask.

Just crossed the floor as if it belonged to her and stopped in front of my desk. She extended a gloved hand, wrist bent like she expected it to be kissed. Long white gloves. Clean and expensive, and a scent that trailed behind her like a whisper from a past life.

Chanel No. 5. Jasmine and sandalwood.
Powder and promise.

She wore a black satin dress that caught the light like moonlight on oil, every curve softened by shadow.

It clung just enough to start rumors and left just enough to keep secrets.

Her heels looked like they'd been forged on the stage of a piano bar at midnight, the kind of place where broken hearts leaned over bourbon and begged for one more song.

And her coat…

Crimson. Draped over her arm like a second skin she hadn't decided whether to shed.

Later, I'd see that coat again in a photograph.
Floating in dark water.
Wrapped around a girl who never had a chance.

But that was after the blood, after the fire, after I'd already made the mistake of thinking I could save her.

My gut told me my world was about to shatter into a thousand pieces.
And she was going to be the one holding the hammer.

"I need you to find someone for me, Mr. Mercer."

I leaned back in my chair, the wood creaking like it had something to say about it.

"Sounds like you already know where she is. Just don't like the view."

She didn't flinch. Just reached into her handbag and pulled out a photograph, sliding it across the desk like it might burn her fingers if she held it any longer.

The girl in the photo looked to be in her mid-twenties. Same jawline. Same fire behind the eyes.

But younger. Softer. Like the city hadn't gotten its claws in her yet.

She could've passed for the woman sitting in front of me if you caught her in the right light. Before the soul got sanded down.

“Slow down, lady.”

I pulled the crumpled pack of Luckies from my coat pocket and gave it a few taps until one slipped out, kissed the corner of my mouth. Scraped a match against the desk.

The flame flared bright, catching the edge of her face, her cheekbones carved from marble, her lips painted in defiance.

I dragged the smoke deep and held it, long enough to let the silence do the talking. That space between breaths? It tells you a lot about a person.

But this one?
I couldn't read a damn thing.

“What's your name, doll?”

The words riding on a wave of smoke.

She let the silence stretch one beat longer than comfort allowed. Then:

“You can call me Angel.”

A grin cracked the left side of my mouth. Just a flicker.

Of course I could.

"The price is two hundred up front, doll. Another two when I find the broad."

I took another drag from the Lucky and let it linger in the air between us.

"But just so we're clear, people don't go missing in this city for no reason. They either don't want to be found… or you're better off not knowing where I dig them up from."

She didn't blink. Just reached into her purse with the kind of grace only money or pain could buy, pulled out a pair of crisp hundreds, and slid them across the desk like they were business cards.

"The money's not a problem," she said. "Find my sister for me, Mr. Mercer."

She didn't wait for me to respond.

Just eased herself around the desk, her heels whispering against the floor, and stopped in front of me.

Both hands rose to my face, gloved fingers

brushing over my three-day stubble like she was memorizing the shape of the damage.

And then.

She kissed me.

A kiss that didn't ask.
A kiss that didn't promise.
A kiss that tasted like trouble, dressed as gratitude.

"I'll leave all the details with your receptionist, Frank."

And just like that, she was gone.

She turned without ceremony, but somehow still made it feel like a curtain call. The hem of that black satin dress caught the light one last time, swaying like smoke from a dying candle.

Her heels struck the floor in measured rhythm, each step softer than the one before, until they faded into the hallway hush.

She didn't look back.

She didn't need to.

The door eased shut behind her with a sigh, not a slam, and the room felt emptier than it had any right to. Her perfume still hung in the air.

Expensive.

With something underneath it... like longing dressed up for a night out.

I sat there a moment, staring at the place she'd just been, wondering if the storm outside had just stepped through my door, or if I'd just offered it a drink and told it my name.

Before I could get too comfortable with my thoughts, the door creaked open again and Rita stepped in, arms crossed, fire already in her eyes.

"The audacity of that woman, Frank. No hello, no waiting, just storms in like she's the Queen of the Goddamn Empire."

I shrugged, still staring at the door she disappeared through.

"Some dames have that quality, baby girl."

Rita snorted, straightened her blouse, and shot me a look that could sand paint off a Buick.

"Yeah, well, I've seen potholes with more class. And I wouldn't trust her as far as I could throw her, and I wear heels, so that ain't far."

A grin crawled up the side of my face, a rare thing these days. Like a sunrise over this God-forsaken city.

"She paid the two hundred up front. I'll find whoever she wants."

Rita shook her head.

Muttered something about fools and easy money, but she didn't push it.

She knew me too well for that.

I stepped back to the window and flicked the old coin into the air, catching it without looking.

Outside, the rain hadn't let up, just like this city, always pouring, always hiding something.

Her silhouette still danced through my mind, all curves and shadows, like a jazz note I couldn't let go of.

I paused for a moment.

Of course her name was Angel.

In this city, it always is.

Chapter 2:
Smoke and Silhouettes

You can smell trouble before you see it. But in a place like the Ember Room, trouble wears heals and sings jazz.

Frank Mercer

I started sifting through the file Angel left with Rita.

Not much to go on.

A couple of train tickets, a worn-out envelope, and a letter written in blue ink with neat, round handwriting, like the kind nuns teach you before the world teaches you better.

"Who in their right mind comes *here* for a visit?" I muttered, flipping the page.

Something near the bottom caught my eye.

"Some things to discuss with Tommy down at the Ember Room."

That name tugged at something in the back of my brain. I studied the photo again.

Fresh-faced. Hopeful. Still believed life owed her something.

The Ember Room wasn't the kind of place for hope. It was high-end, slick, all chrome and crimson velvet.

The kind of place where favors were traded in whispers, and souls were bartered behind drawn curtains.

What was a wide-eyed out-of-towner doing in a place like *that*?

I glanced at the stack of files on my desk, missing persons, faded ink and broken dreams. In this city, they go missing by the dozen.

Most wind up in the river, tangled in secrets or swimming in regret. Sometimes they just flew too close to something bright and burned all the way down.

I decided I'd pay the Ember Room a visit tonight. Maybe I'd go in. Maybe I'd watch from the shadows. Depends how the wind blows.

It was dark. The kind of dark that swallowed street corners whole.

The city lights pulsed with the nervous twitch of flickering streetlamps, like they weren't sure if they wanted to show up tonight.
Neon signs bled color into the puddles, painting everything in red, blue, and bad decisions.

I stood under an awning across the street,
collar up.

Flipping my father's old coin in the air and
catching it without breaking my stare.

Cigarette burning down in the other.

Let's see who walks in.
Let's see who doesn't come back out.

The Ember Room started filling with the usual
suspects, low-level mob guys in slick suits that
cost more than their lives.

They talk too much, die too fast, and never
seem to learn the difference.

Then the city men arrive, officials with smiles
too wide, hands too clean. And trailing behind
them, the high-society dreamers from the
outskirts.

They come here looking to sell their souls in
exchange for a little attention. A little affection,
a little hope that maybe their tomorrow won't
look like their yesterday.

That's when I saw him.

Bannon.

My old sergeant from the force. The man who taught me how to survive the streets, before I outed him and his buddies for playing dirty with the city's backroom games.

Turns out the city was in on it too. Judges, councilmen, even the damn mayor's office. Bannon didn't fall. He was caught.

I made my way over into the crowded wait line, keeping a distance.

I waited. Watched him disappear into the red-drenched crowd, schmoozing like nothing ever stuck to him. When he's gone, I make my move.

The Ember Room was exactly what you'd expect: red velvet lounges that look soft but never forgive, drapes thick enough to muffle sins, and chandeliers that drip light like melting gold.

The walls hum with jazz, low and smoky, the type of music that makes you feel like something's about to happen.

Or already did.

There's perfume in the air and sweat under the collars. Everything smells like money trying to cover up fear.

I make my way to the bar.

"Bourbon," I tell the bartender. "Two fingers. No ice."

He nods without a word and slides it across.

The first sip burns like an old memory, sharp, warm, and a little bitter. Just how I like it.

I hear the announcer crackle over the crowd, half-swallowed by clinking glasses and whispered deals.

"Now introducing… the lovely Miss Angel Devine."

And there she was.

All satin and no mercy.

She stepped into the spotlight like she owned the moonlight it was borrowed from.

That crimson coat draped over her shoulders,

same one I saw folded on my desk, same one in the photo floating in black water.

She peeled it off slow, like a curtain on a final act, revealing a dress that could bring kings to their knees and sinners to church.

Black, smooth, poured on her like midnight oil. The sort of dress that made promises it had no intention of keeping.

The crowd hushed the way a crowd only does when danger takes the mic.

And then she sang.

Her tone like smoke through a keyhole.

Low.

Breathy.

The sound of heartbreak hiding behind red lipstick. Every note carved the air open like it remembered pain and wasn't ready to forget.

I took a long sip of my bourbon and didn't blink.

Because right then, I realized something.

This case wasn't about finding a missing girl.
It was about following the one in the crimson coat…
and hoping to hell I didn't lose myself along the way.

I made my way toward the stage like I was caught in a trance.

Could've been the bourbon.

Could've been the way she curled around my spine.

But it was her eyes, locked on mine like she already knew how the story ended.

Angel stepped off the stage mid-verse, note never wavering, heels clicking in time with the band.

She drifted through the crowd like silk poured over glass.

No one moved to stop her.

Not even the band.

Then she was in front of me.

One hand, gloved, satin, deliberate, brushed against my face as she sang the last note into my ear. A soft caress that lingered longer than it should've.

The room sat still.

Watching her.

As though they had forgotten how to breathe.

I took a long sip of bourbon, like I was still playing it cool.

But she had me.
And she knew it.

She turned and sauntered through the crowd. Giving just enough attention to the men who thought they mattered.

After the song ended and the applause faded into chatter, I peeled myself off the floor and wandered back to the bar.

Time to stop watching the fire and start poking it.

I slipped the bartender a ten,
I let it settle.
A bribe dressed as a tip.

"I've got questions," I said. "Some about the lady, for personal reasons. Some about a guy named Tommy."

He glanced around, then leaned in, wiping the counter more out of habit than necessity.

"Tommy Ricci," he muttered.

"Up-and-comer. Mob's got their hooks deep into him.
If he makes it through his initiation, he'll be trouble."

He nodded toward the far side of the room.

That's when I saw him.

Tommy was built like a prizefighter with something to prove.

Lean, sharp-dressed, jaw tight like he ground his teeth in his sleep.

He didn't look around much.

Men like him don't need to.

I made my way over, dropped into the seat across from him, and lit a cigarette, adding smoke to a room already drowning in it.

"You must be Tommy," I said.

His head lifted.

Face tightened .

He looked like a man chewing on broken glass.

He was working out my angle, friend, threat, or something worse.

"Relax," I added, "just need to ask a few questions."

He leaned back, arms crossed, half yelling over the music.

"I don't talk to cops."

"Good," I said, exhaling a lazy stream of smoke, "neither do I."

"I'm looking for someone," I said across the table, low but firm.

My thumb found the gold crown of my wristwatch and rolled it back and forth.

Habit more than necessity.

"Word is, she was headed here to talk to you about something."

Tommy didn't blink. Just leaned back in his seat, arms draped across the booth like he owned the leather.

"I talk to a lot of people… Mister."
He let the silence hang, smoke curling from his cigar like punctuation.

"Mercer. Frank Mercer. Private Investigator."

A flicker of recognition in his expression.

Not much, but enough.

"Oh yeah," he said, lips curling.

 "Nice to put a face to the name."

Turns out when you start solving high-profile cases in a city built on secrets, folks start to notice. Whether that's a good thing or a death sentence, well, that part's still playing out.

"Who you lookin' for, Mr. Mercer?" he asked, voice gravel-worn from shouting over music and breathing secondhand sins.

"City's full of missing girls. Gotta be more specific."

"A young lady named Marcy," I replied. "She was on her way here to meet with you. Said there were things to discuss."

He raised an eyebrow, exchanged a glance with the goons flanking him.

"Marcy, huh?" He chuckled.

"Don't know no Marcys. But for the right price, I could introduce you to a few girls who'd *say* they're Marcy, if that's what gets you outta bed in the morning."

His crew laughed like hyenas trying out for cabaret.

I didn't.

My voice dropped low, stern, flat.

The type of tone that ends conversations or starts something worse.

"That joke ain't gonna land, Mr. Ricci."

The laughter stopped cold. I crushed my cigarette into the ashtray in front of me, the hiss of it louder than the band for a moment.

"And I don't appreciate the insinuations."

"So tell me again, Frank, who's this broad you're looking for?"

"Her name's Marcy," I said. "Don't know much else. She caught the bus in from outta town. Said she was coming here to see you."

I slid the photograph across the table.

Tommy picked it up, gave it a glance that lasted longer than it needed to.

"Pretty girl," he muttered. "Who's paying you to find her?"

"I can't tell you that," I said, and let my eyes drift toward the stage. Just long enough for him to follow the trail.

His expression hardened.
He got the message.

"I see," he said, sitting back and giving me the full once-over while sipping his bourbon.

He was weighing me, the job, and the strings attached.

"Say I *did* know something about this Marcy… what's in it for me?"

I tilted my head, half a grin pulled at the corner of my mouth.

"Maybe the person who hired me would be… grateful for your help. Grateful in a way that matters."

His eyes lit up for a second, glint of interest, flicker of greed, but it didn't last.
He sank back into the booth.

As if the weight of the world caught up with him.

"Alright, Mr. Mercer," he said.

His expression darkened.

"Just know this, my information ain't free. And it sure as hell don't come cheap."

He leaned in, smoke curling between us like a warning.

"One day there'll be a price to pay. You understand?"

I nodded, not because I agreed, because I'd already added it to the tab.

"The girl was headed here," Tommy said, leaning across the table on one arm.

Just far enough to make me lean in.

"Because moves are bein' made at the club. Quiet ones. Smart ones. Somebody up north wanted to know who was stirring the pot."

He tapped the photo with one finger.

"She had a reputation. Marcy wasn't just some skirt on a sightseeing trip."

He glanced around the room.

"She was the kind of broad who'd give you the night of your life... then plant a stiletto through your spine before the sun came up."

I raised an eyebrow, kept my face neutral. "Did you get to meet with her?"

He shook his head.

"Nah. She never showed. Was supposed to meet me two nights ago. Thought maybe she got spooked... or maybe she already found what she was looking for."

He paused, took another sip.

"Now I gotta figure out what the boys up north are gonna do when their girl doesn't come home."

I leaned back slightly, letting the weight of that land.

Marcy wasn't missing.

She was gone.

And whoever sent her wasn't going to light candles and say prayers.

They were going to ask questions, send people, and make examples.

The picture on my desk just got a whole a lot heavier.

Chapter 3:
What the Water Remembers

You throw enough bodies in the river; it starts whispering names.

Frank Mercer

I stood under the front awning of the Ember Room, the velvet rope swaying in the rain.

I pulled the pack of Lucky Strikes from my coat pocket, tapped one loose, and placed it between my lips.

A scratch of the match flared orange, casting a flicker of life in a city that forgot how to breathe.

The meeting with Tommy went better than expected. No concrete lead yet, but information.

The type of information that burrows into your brain and starts rearranging things.

I started the long walk back to the office. The rain had lightened to a soft patter, tapping on my shoulders like a gentle reminder of past mistakes.

Tommy didn't mince words.

Marcy wasn't the lamb Angel made her out to be.

She was the wolf.

A girl with teeth behind that smile. Sent here to sniff out power plays and maybe bite down if she had to.

The smoke curled around my fingers as I walked.

A ghost drifting through the night, unaware it was already dead.

I stepped over a crumbling pothole, water slick and shining like old blood in the blinking neon.

But what troubled me more than Marcy was Angel.

Why sell her sister as a victim? Surely she knew what kind of woman Marcy really was. So why lie?

Unless she was playing me, too.

I thought back to the night at the Ember Room. Every time I glanced her way, our eyes met. Not once. *Every single time.*

That wasn't coincidence.
That was surveillance.
She was watching me. Watching Tommy.
Closer than she ever let on.

The next morning, the lights in the office flickered four or five times before they clunked to life, humming like they weren't happy about it.

I lifted my head from the couch, the leather creaking beneath me, and saw Rita standing in the doorway holding a fresh cup of coffee.

"Thanks, baby girl," I muttered.

Running my hands down my face.

"Smells better than usual this morning."

She arched her brow.

"Yeah, well, figured I'd spare you the swamp water you usually call coffee. You're welcome."

The phone had been ringing off and on for the last twenty minutes, like it knew I was ignoring it on purpose.

"Any chance you're gonna answer that today, Rita?" I asked, half into my first sip.

She spun on her heel like a dancer at closing time, hair whipping over her shoulder.

"Any chance you're gonna get off that couch and do something besides drink and brood?" she shot back.

I huffed through my nose into my cup.

She always knew where to land the punch.

She disappeared through the door, heels clicking out into the front room. A few minutes passed before she bustled back in, more urgency in her step than usual.

"It's Murph, Frank. Said he heard you were asking around about the girl from out of town."

I sat up straighter, the grin fading.
"Yeah? What's Murph got to say?"

"She's dead, Frank."

That landed hard.

"He wants to meet you down by the docks in a half hour."

I exhaled through my nose, slow and bitter.

"Figures, no one who goes missing in this town wants to be found."

I reached for my coat and lit a Lucky off the stove burner.

"And if they were, they usually floated to the surface on their own."

The docks smelled like you'd think; only worse. Add a few-day-old body to the stew and let it simmer in diesel, rot, and bad decisions, and things go stale real fast.

The kind of stale that clings to your coat and follows you home.

I found Murph where he always was, half in shadow, half in something stronger.

We exchanged a nod and skipped the small talk.

He glanced around like the fish might be listening, then slipped a file from the inside of his coat and handed it off quiet-like.

"Word is you've been asking around about this one," he muttered.

"Figured I'd give you a heads-up before you get blindsided. She's not your usual floater, Frank."

"She's connected," I said.

Murph shook his head.

"Not just connected."

"*Deep* connected."

"The kind of roots that grow beneath the concrete."

He adjusted his fedora slightly while looking to see who might be listening.

"She was sent down to clean up a mess at the Ember Room, don't know who or what, but it wasn't gonna end pretty."

I opened the file, black-and-white photos, coroner notes, a name that already felt too heavy.

Marcy Devine.

"How'd she die?"

"Strangled," Murph said.

"Strangled."

"Clean job. Whatever they used cut deep."

He paused.

"Left a line around her throat like somebody drew it with a razor."

"Real clean. No hesitation marks. Then they dumped her in the river like she was yesterday's headline."

I reached up and slid the knot of my tie from around my neck.

I stared down at the photo, Marcy's face pale, lips slightly parted, as if death caught her mid-word.

And that crimson coat, soaked, wrapped around her like a goodbye.

This wasn't a warning. It was a message.

And I was already too deep to walk away.

Back at the office.

I sat at my desk.

Watching the worn down old coin flip from finger to finger.

The hum of the city was distant now, muted by cracked glass and old regrets.

I pulled out my notepad and started scribbling, thumb flicking through the folder Murph passed off at the docks.

The pages were damp with river stink and something worse, stale coffee, old bourbon, and the weight of truth trying to stay buried.

The room smelled like the past. And I was sitting in the middle of it.

Then I saw it.

A photograph, half-tucked beneath a pile of handwritten police notes, edges curled and stained.

The coat.

Knee-length. Tie front. Velvet.

Looked like it was made for the girl in it, Marcy. It suited her.

Framed her just right.

But it suited *Angel* better.

She was wearing it the day she walked into my office, perfume first and lies second. The red velvet draped over her arm like an afterthought.

I sat back in my chair, the realization tightening in my chest.

That meant Angel had seen Marcy after she arrived, or someone close enough to Marcy had passed the coat along. Either way, Angel had lied.

Angel didn't just know her sister was in town. She saw her.

And she didn't say a damn thing.

Pieces of Angel were starting to fall into place. The damsel in distress who loved the spotlight but pulled every string behind the curtain.

The question wasn't *where* Marcy went. It was *why* Angel sent me to look for a girl she already knew was dead.

She was just a singer at the club, at least, that's how she played it. But singers don't wear their dead sister's coat like a trophy.

The questions started piling up like bodies in the river.

And I wasn't going to find any answers sitting here breathing in the ghosts of last week's bourbon.

The door burst open and Rita stormed in. Her hands on her hips, lipstick sharp enough to cut glass.

"I gotta get back down there," I muttered. "Talk to Angel."

Rita crossed her arms, not bothering to hide the look that said *I told you so*.

"I warned you, Frank. That girl's trouble wrapped in velvet. You let her in too deep, she'll have you under her thumb 'til the day you forget your own name."

I smirked, grabbed my coat.

"Yours is the only thumb I'm under, Rita."

She rolled her eyes, but the corner of her mouth betrayed her, half a smile in full red.

"Damn right," she said. "Now go get lied to again, sweetheart. Just don't forget who's

gonna be here with black coffee and peroxide
when it all blows up."

Chapter 4:
The Weight of Red

You chase ghosts long enough, you start seeing your reflection in the dirt they left behind.

Frank Mercer

I spent the day chasing down leads for other clients, stolen money, cheating husbands, lies dressed in silk and guilt.

The usual noise.

The bills don't stop just because I'm in too deep on another case.

They don't care who's dead, who's lying, or who's dancing in velvet with blood on her heels.

That evening, I took myself back down to the Ember Room.

Chase a few leads.

Drink a bourbon. See who crawled out tonight.

The city was dressed in its usual attire; smog wrapped in satin and lipstick, the kind of evening better through a glass than a windshield.

Rain kept falling. Steady. Soft. Just enough to rinse the blood off the sidewalks without anyone noticing.

The Ember Room hummed the way it always did. Low jazz. Dim lights. Deals being made between clinks of glass and half-finished promises.

Angel was on stage.
She wore midnight blue, tight at the waist, soft at the edges.

The sort of dress that whispered danger in all the right places.

A slit up one leg gave the piano player a reason to play slower.

 Her hair was pinned up, curls cascading just enough to tease the back of her neck.

She sang low, like she knew secrets the rest of us had to pay for.

None of the usual suspects were around. No Tommy. No Bannon. Just smoke, saxophone, and side glances.

I ordered my usual, bourbon, two fingers, no ice, and slid into a seat at the bar.

Let's see who shows up.

The night was dragging its heels, but the crowd had started to swell, cigars lit, laughter getting looser, and the bourbon burning warmer with each pour.

I was three drinks deep when the room erupted into a standing ovation.

Angel had finished her first set.

She stepped off the stage.
Graceful and deliberate.

Soaking in the applause like it was the crown she'd always deserved.

She didn't smile.
She didn't need to.

She floated through the room like gravity had given her the night off.

A few minutes later, a soft hand touched my shoulder, gloved fingers brushing the fabric of my coat like a secret.

"Frank," she whispered, just close enough to taste the smoke on my collar.

"Come to my room in five minutes… I've got something to show you."

By the time I turned, all I saw was the sway of her hips vanishing into the crowd.

Questions started lining up in my head like suspects.
Was I getting too close?
Was she playing games again, here, in her own house?

I gave it five. Then knocked once and invited myself in.

There she was, standing in front of the vanity, an angel in a silk slip, and nothing left to the imagination. It shimmered in the low light, hugging her like a secret.

She drifted toward me like she'd already decided how the night would end.

Wrapped her arms around my neck, and kissed me deep. A kiss that didn't ask permission. The kind that says you're not in charge anymore.

She pulled away, just enough to breathe against my cheek.

"Frank… things are changing. Fast. I don't know what's coming tomorrow. Tonight… tonight's just for us."

A slight pull tugging at the left corner of my mouth.

"Sure thing, doll."

I shrugged out of my trench coat and tossed it onto the chair.

Right next to the crimson coat.

It sat there, folded, silent, soaked in memory.

I stared at it for a second too long.

Then Angel pulled me back in.

I walked out a little while later, shirt still wrinkled from sins not yet confessed. The club had changed while I was gone, more crowded now, noisier, meaner somehow.

A thick layer of smoke drifted across the ceiling like a second story waiting to collapse.

That's when I saw Tommy.

He was stiff, posture tight.
His jaw tightened around a thought he didn't

like.

His hands did the talking, quick, sharp gestures. Heated.

I couldn't see who he was barking at.

Until I got closer.

Bannon.

Of course it was Bannon.

I slipped into the edge of the conversation like a shadow with a smirk.

"Well, look who it is. Thought I smelled cheap cologne and corruption."

Bannon turned, red already rising in his face.

"Frank," he growled. "I told you to stay the hell away from here. You must be dumber than a box of rocks."

I grinned, the kind you wear when you've already won the hand and everyone else is still playing.

"Sorry, Red. Guess I was distracted. Hard to keep track of time when you're spending the evening wrapped in velvet and lipstick."

That landed hard. The whole city knows about Bannon's obsession with Angel.

Tommy coughed into his drink, trying not to laugh.

Bannon didn't smile.

He didn't blink either.

I had his attention now.

"You find out anything else about Marcy, Frank?" Tommy asked, low and even.

"If I did," I said, flicking ash into an empty glass.

"I wouldn't be saying it around this guy. The trail would go cold faster than a body in the river."

Bannon didn't like that. He never did.

He grabbed me by the collar, again. Like it ever worked.

Before I could respond, Tommy stepped in, hand on Bannon's arm.

"Easy," he said, demeanor calm but full of weight.

Bannon hesitated. Then let go, jaw tight, temper burning.

"I see who you're aligning yourself with now, Frank," he sneered. "From police to crook."

"Better than staying just a crooked cop, Red."

He stormed off like a man who knew the walls were starting to close in.

I turned back to Tommy.

"Marcy was here, alright. She floated to the surface yesterday."

Tommy's face clenched for half a second. That was all.

"Angel told me things were changing around here," I added. "Any idea what she meant?"

He didn't answer right away. Just stared past me, like something dark had walked into the room that no one else could see.

"All I know is… that's who she was coming to talk to me about."

"She was coming to talk about Angel?"

"Yeah. Girl's been climbing the ladder on her own.

Fast.

Real fast.
The bosses don't like that."

He paused, eyes flicking toward the dressing rooms.

"And I ain't crossing her, Frank. Not for anyone."

I made my way back to Angel's dressing room and knocked once before letting myself in.

She didn't even turn to look.

"You're not ready again, are you, Frank?" she said, teasing, silk slip barely hanging on.

"A night like that usually takes a man a few days to recover."

She wasn't wrong.
And she knew it.

The crimson coat caught my sight, hanging on the back of the chair like it was watching me.

I moved around the dressing room while we spoke.

Dresses hung from brass hooks along the wall.

Sheet music sat scattered across a side table.

Instruments lined the far corner.

And on the dresser...

Lengths of piano wire.

Neat silver coils.

Thin.

Strong.

Clean enough to cut deep.

Like a razor.

Murph's words drifted back to me from the docks.

Left a line around her throat like somebody drew it with a razor.

"Tell me, Angel."

"Where'd you get the coat?"

"Oh, it was just a gift from an old friend," she said, smooth as silk.

Like she'd rehearsed that line in the mirror a thousand times.

"I didn't get the chance to tell you," I said.

Watching her eyes more than her lips.

"I found your sister."

A blink. That was it.

Her face didn't flinch.

Not even a twitch.

"She came up for air yesterday."

Her hands went to her mouth like she was shocked.

"No…" she whispered, hand to her mouth. Her eyes stayed dry.

"Strangled," I added.

She slumped into my arms, let out a soft whimper. I'd heard that sound from dames a hundred times.

It always meant the same thing... nothing.

"You said things were changing," I pressed.

"Does it have anything to do with the girl the boys up north sent down to clean up the mess?"

She straightened, brushed imaginary dust from her slip.

"Oh, Frank... you don't need to worry about her," she said.

"You don't need to worry about Marcy anymore, Frank."

"That situation has passed."

She turned toward the vanity, smiling at her reflection.

"The Ember Room is mine now."

I stepped back.
"The Ember Room... is yours?" That hit hard, like a punch in the gut.

She walked over, pulled me close, kissed me again. I didn't pull away.
Couldn't. Or maybe I just didn't want to.

"The Ember Room needs someone who can survive it," she whispered.

I let the kiss break, my hands tightening around her arms.

"Did you kill her, Angel?"

She didn't answer. Just turned back to the mirror, kept fixing her lipstick for the next set.

I grabbed her shoulders and spun her around.

"Did you kill your sister, Angel? I saw the coat. I know it's hers."

My voice was low. Stern. Like judgment waiting for confession.

The corner of her mouth twitched.

Not a lot.

But enough.

Carrying the quiet confidence of a loaded revolver.

"Relax, Frank. I didn't kill her."

"Then how'd you end up with her coat?"

"It was a gift," she said, without blinking.

"You seem to get a lot of gifts, Angel."

She leaned in close, just enough to feel the heat of her breath.

"When you know the right people, Frank…"

She paused, lips curling at the edge.

"The cards fall your way."

I left the room without another word.
She didn't stop me. She didn't have to.

I made my way to the bar and ordered a bourbon, neat, strong, fast. Let it burn the taste of her out of my mouth.
Didn't work.

The crowd stirred behind me, then rose to their feet as the announcer took the mic.

"Ladies and gentlemen… Miss Angel Devine, for her final performance of the night."

She stepped out from behind the velvet curtain like a queen returning to her court. Glamorous as always.
Dressed to kill.

And this time… in a crimson coat.

The same coat her sister died in.
And now it wore her like it was always meant to.

Angel shimmered under the spotlight.

The crowd hung on every sway of her hips, every note she poured into the room.

No one in that room knew what she was capable of.

I was starting to.

Angel didn't just survive the Ember Room.
She owned it now.

I leaned against the bar and rolled the
coin across my fingers while I watched
from the shadows.

She was dangerous.

I knew it the same way a man knows when the
bullet's already left the barrel.

But proof?

Proof would've made it real.

And maybe I wasn't ready for that.

Some dames dance through the fire.

Angel made it her stage.

Final Thoughts:

By the time the curtain fell, she owned the
room, the coat, and maybe even me.
I knew enough. Enough to stop. I didn't.
The truth was bleeding through. I just kept
wiping my hands clean.

That's the thing about devils in red.
They don't ask for your soul.
You give it to them, willingly.

And the worst part?
That was just the beginning.

When Angels Bleed… I'll be there to watch.

Frank W Mercer

Thank you for your support

If you've made it this far, you've got a stronger stomach than most folks in this city.

Thanks for stepping into the shadows with me and digging through the lies.

If you're hungry for more cases, or you want to hear my voice telling it like it is, come join me on YouTube at:
 http://www.youtube.com/@TheMercerFiles

Hit that like and subscribe button, helps keep the lights on and the bourbon flowing.

Or feel Free to "Buy Me a Coffee" from
coff.ee/TheMercerFiles

Stay tuned for Season Two. Coming Soon.

Some stories don't end. They just wait for the next page.

Want to watch these episodes?

Follow each episode on our Youtube channel.

Scan me!

Copyright Page

The Mercer Files: Season One
© 2026 Phillip Deam

First published 2026
Australia

ISBN: 978-1-7642123-2-8

Cover design and interior design by the author.